A SHIFTER CHRISTMAS CAROL

SHIFTERS UNBOUND

JENNIFER ASHLEY

JA / AG PUBLISHING

A Shifter Christmas Carol

Shifters Unbound

Cover design by Kim Killion

CHAPTER ONE

"Dylan isn't coming."

Glory's voice floated up the stairs from the kitchen to the bedroom where Dylan packed the few belongings he'd need.

He heard her simmering rage from their hours-long argument they'd had in the back yard, Glory letting forth at the top of her voice. Dylan had answered more quietly but just as adamantly.

He hadn't won the argument—exactly. Glory had simply stalked off, every gorgeous inch of her tight with fury. She'd learned when to give up on Dylan.

One day, Dylan knew, she might keep walking and not come back. Or at least kick him the hell out. He lived in her house.

He stashed small knives and other sharp objects into his backpack among his clothes. Dylan rarely relied on weapons, as his Shifter cat was a better weapon than anything forged, but sometimes the enemies he faced fought dirty, and he didn't always have time to shift.

"Not coming?" Andrea, Dylan's daughter-in-law, asked in surprise. "To the Yule celebration—none of it?"

"He's heading to New Orleans." Glory spoke steadily, but Dylan heard the effort that took. "Contacts to see. Arrangements to make."

Sean, Dylan's son, broke in. "He can't be meeting Shifters, then. They'll be at their own Yule celebrations."

"You heard me." Glory's heels clicked as she moved across the room below. "He's your dad, Sean. You know better than most he does what he damn well pleases."

Andrea broke in. "Do you want me to talk to him?"

Dylan quickly threw the last of his things together. He could easily stave off Sean, and even his oldest son, Liam, technically Dylan's clan leader now, but Andrea was a different matter.

Andrea was a half-Fae, half-wolf Shifter, and when she looked at Dylan with her clear gray eyes, he felt her power, the deep magic of her Fae ancestry. Andrea was a gentle soul and would hurt no one—that is, no one except any who threatened Sean or her son—but she had a way of getting inside a man's head to make him speak the truth.

"No," Glory said sharply. "Let him go. I don't give a shit what he does."

Sean and Andrea went silent. They'd learned not to interfere in an argument between Dylan and Glory. Fur would fly—literally.

Dylan hoisted his pack, zipped his thick jacket, and left the room, moving swiftly down the stairs. The bungalow had an open floor plan, so he couldn't depart by either front door or back without being seen. Only climbing out the window would let him leave surreptitiously, but Dylan was in no mood for scrambling across roofs.

He felt four pairs of eyes on him as he stepped off the stairs and headed for the front door—Glory, Sean, Andrea, and Sean and Andrea's cub, Kenny, who was all of two years old. They watched him in silence, the adults in various stages of anger, Kenny without expression.

Kenny, Dylan's beloved grandson, could be as unnerving as his mother. He was one-quarter Fae, three-quarters Shifter, and had inherited Andrea's dark hair and gray eyes.

They were wolf's eyes. While Shifter cubs of mixed ancestry did not show their animal forms until they were about three years old, Dylan had no doubt that Kenny would be wolf. Sean and family were Feline—black-maned lions—but Kenny already had the unnervingly patient stare of a large gray wolf.

The lad seemed to know about things before they happened and could look at a man with a canny understanding far older than his physical age. The next moment, he'd be a normal cub, running with his cousins and screaming as loudly as any of them.

"I'll be back as soon as I can," Dylan said to the silence.

"Do you need me to come with you, Dad?" Sean asked. He was offering backup, in case any of Dylan's contacts turned violent. Sean knew better than most what kinds of beings Dylan had dealt with in the past.

"And have Andrea tear out my guts?" Dylan answered, not entirely joking. "Glory's already in line for that, and I need some of my insides to stay with me. Don't worry, son. Ben will be there."

Sean relaxed slightly and gave him a nod. Ben was the best kind of backup. "The Goddess go with you."

The ladies and Kenny said nothing at all. Glory, dressed in skintight black pants and a silver top, turned her golden head away and wouldn't look at him. Andrea and Kenny kept up the scary gray-eyed stares.

"Goddess go with you," Dylan said to them all, and left the house.

He stashed his pack in the saddlebag of his motorcycle and straddled the seat. Liam came out onto the porch next door in a T-shirt and jeans, barefoot. It was in the 70s today, December 20, though it was supposed to drop into the 40s tomorrow and possibly snow. That was Austin for you.

"This is important, is it?" Liam asked. Even he didn't know what the meeting was about, but he accepted it with a bit more understanding than the others.

"It is."

"Yule is sacred, you know."

Dylan did know that, but their enemies didn't give a rat's ass what was sacred to Shifters. "It was now or never, son. I'll try to make it quick."

Liam didn't believe him, any more than Glory had. The meeting Dylan had set up might lead to more, which meant he could be gone for a week, or weeks.

But that was the way things were. Dylan was fighting a war—a war Shifters had to win or they'd be wiped out of existence. His family didn't always understand exactly what Dylan had to do to keep them safe. And it was better they didn't—knowing too much would be dangerous for them.

Dylan's days as clan leader, and Shiftertown leader, were behind him, though he'd never walk away from protecting not only his family but all Shifters. Glory knew that, and his priorities sometimes made her bitter. Dylan was surprised she'd stayed with him this long—she was constantly pissed off at him.

Dylan started the motorcycle, lifted a hand to Liam, who returned the gesture, and rode from the driveway to the quiet Shiftertown street.

Evidence of the coming Yule celebration met him everywhere—streamers hung from trees, white lights twinkled on houses, small bonfires had already begun in open areas. On one corner, Ronan, in his Kodiak bear form, had harnessed himself to the giant Yule log and was dragging it toward the common area where they'd decorate and light it.

Ronan's bear face wore irritation, because every cub around had jumped onto the log to catch a ride. Spike, the all-tattooed jaguar Shifter, guided the log, but didn't chase the cubs away. Spike's mate, Myka, seemed to be giving directions, and both men were growling. Not that this disturbed Myka, who was used to wrangling stubborn animals.

Dylan rode past without stopping. If he was pulled into conversation with every Shifter he passed he'd never get free of Shiftertown.

Was that what he wanted? He rode out of the open chain-link gate, exited Shiftertown, and made his way past the bar to Airport Boulevard. Freedom from Shiftertown?

Of course he did—he wanted all Shifters to tear off

their shock Collars and live anywhere they pleased, not only in the mandated housing in Shiftertowns. To work at any job they liked, travel anywhere they wanted without having to obtain permission. But Dylan also wanted Shifters to stay together, as clans, families, friends. They were stronger together.

So why did he always breathe a sigh of relief when he was alone on the open road?

Because out here no one questioned him, second-guessed him, or tried to stop him. Dylan had to make hard choices, unpopular ones, but they were necessary. Easier to make those decisions on his own, far from his family and almost-mate, Glory. Sean and Liam could argue the hind leg off a donkey. Dylan was glad he'd raised strong sons, but Goddess help him, they defied him right and left.

There were things Dylan had to do. Ugly things, violent things. Dylan did them because no one else would.

He crouched over the bike and opened it up when he hit the highway out of town. Sweet release. The wind had turned cold by the time he reached the junction of the I-10 and headed toward Houston, New Orleans waiting beyond it.

———

THE HOUSE A FEW MILES OUTSIDE NEW ORLEANS, where the strange being who called himself Ben waited, was haunted. Or at least, that was the rumor. The house pretty much decided what it wanted people to think about it.

Dylan arrived well after dark. He'd stopped only once on the road to relieve himself, and he was due again—so he pounded rather impatiently on the door.

"Come on, lad." Dylan put his hand on the door-frame when all his knocking produced no results. "I'm not growing any younger out here."

The latch clicked, and the door creaked open. Dylan slid quickly inside, ignoring the door that slammed itself shut, bolts sliding into place on their own.

He ran lightly up the stairs and to the bathroom, tossing his pack into the bedroom he'd used before. By the time he'd washed up, running a hand through his dark hair to tidy it—avoiding looking at the gray in it—he realized how empty the house was.

"You here, Ben?" he called down the silent corri-dor, but he knew he was alone.

The house smelled empty, missing Ben's unique scent—a bite of mint and brimstone that Shifters often mistook for Fae. Ben was a creature who'd originated in Faerie, but he definitely wasn't Fae, and made sure everyone knew it.

Dylan let out a noise of irritation and moved down the hall to the kitchen to put together a snack from the well-stocked refrigerator. The kitchen was on the second floor, because the first floor was a perfectly preserved antebellum house, shown to tourists several days a week. The woman who owned the house, Jasmine, now the mate of a Shifter, allowed Shifters to use the place anytime they wanted, as long as they kept it clean. Ben, who loved a good haunted house, had moved in to be its caretaker.

Dylan ate his sandwich, washed down with a bottle of Guinness, checked the house for security—it had locked itself up tight—and went to bed. He'd have a long day tomorrow, and he needed to be rested to face the beings he'd agreed to meet.

The silence and darkness was unusual. Dylan's life abounded with noise—Sean and Andrea laughing and talking, arguing or making up; Glory either raging or in high spirits; Liam, Kim and family walking into the house any time, with Dylan's grandson Connor who couldn't stay silent if his life depended on it. Sometimes they'd bring Tiger and his voluble mate, Carly, along with their cub and now the daughter Tiger had discovered he had only a few months ago.

The quiet pressed on him. Dylan ignored it. He needed the peace to gear up for tomorrow. No interruptions. No yelling. No humans from Shifter Bureau showing up to make snap inspections. No noise at all.

He drifted to sleep.

He woke when the ceiling above him plunged downward, coming straight for him, led by the heavy iron chandelier. Dylan was halfway out of the bed with the speed of his wildcat, diving to the floor.

Too late. The bulk of the ceiling, weighted by the chandelier, crashed down on him, crushing him whole.

Dylan lay faceup and paralyzed, not breathing, not living, but curiously not dying either.

As his brain tried to figure out what parts of his body, if any, still worked, a giant, misshapen hand wrapped itself around one of the heavy beams and tossed it aside.

CHAPTER TWO

The hand shrunk into a human shape, three of its fingers tattooed with letters that spelled out *Ben*.

Dylan tried to let out a breath of relief and realized he couldn't. His chest had stopped moving, his heart had ceased beating. Yet he could clearly see the square face of Ben and his liquid brown eyes peering over the rubble.

"Sorry about this," Ben said as he moved another beam with unholy strength. "Happens sometimes. Sucks, but it does."

"Ceiling falling in?"

Dylan heard the question, but his lips hadn't formed it. His voice echoed outside his body, and Ben heard it too.

"Suspended animation," Ben answered. "You're meant to stay put."

"The house did this?"

"Who the hell knows? All I know is you're here and you're stuck with me while I take you on a journey."

"What journey?" Dylan scowled, or attempted to. "We're meeting the *zilithal* tomorrow. If I don't show up, a year of planning goes down the drain. I need their intel."

"Yeah, well, if it was up to me, I'd be in the kitchen downing beer and watching TV. I'm behind on *The Crown*."

"Go watch. I'll sleep—once I get out from under this."

"No, my friend. You aren't going anywhere."

Dylan topped Ben by a foot—when Dylan could stand. Even in his three hundredth year, having borne three sons who had children of their own, Dylan had more strength and fight in him than most Shifters. He battled at the fight club to keep himself in shape, and he could beat all but a few.

But whenever Ben lost his stupid grin and pinned you with his dark stare, you felt his power. Dylan had never attempted to best him, and he didn't want to try now.

"I'm obviously going nowhere," Dylan said. "Do what you want."

"OK." Ben reached for him. "I have to hold your hand. Don't take it the wrong way."

Shifters didn't have a problem with touch—they needed it, in fact, to survive—but Dylan jumped when Ben's hand contacted his. Ben's power sparked and sizzled, showing Dylan that this ancient being had far more to him than anyone understood.

"You might want to close your eyes for this," Ben said as his fingers clamped down. "I know I do. Makes me motion sick. No? All right then—here we *go*."

Dylan regretted in the next second that his eyes refused to close.

The world spun, the house vanishing to be replaced by whirling stars and freezing cold. Nausea bit at him, bile rushing to his mouth. His uncooperative throat wouldn't let him release it or cough it back down.

Darkness consumed them, and the cold only built. Damned unfair that Dylan could still feel when he couldn't move. His only contact with reality—if it was reality—was the warmth of Ben's hard hand.

After what seemed hours, the earth slammed up into them, and the spinning ceased.

The cold worsened, and Dylan understood why in

a few seconds. They were no longer in southern Louisiana.

Damp coated the dark air, bringing a chill that penetrated to his bones. The ground was soft, the sort of ground that never quite dried. Dylan scented peat, mud, mist, and grass—scents he hadn't smelled since ...

"What the fuck are we doing in Ireland?"

Dylan's mouth moved that time, and his lungs worked. He breathed out, coughing at last, and spit bile into the grass.

"Is that where this is?" Ben glanced around with interest. "Looks dark."

"Shouldn't be, if it's well past midnight in New Orleans. Six hour time difference." Darkness lingered at the winter solstice, of course, but they should at least glimpse a dawn sky.

"Doesn't mean we're here at the same time, if you catch my drift," Ben said.

Dylan yanked his hand from Ben's and straightened up, stretching his back. His bones didn't feel broken or even bruised. Out-of-body experience? Dream?

This felt too real to be a dream. He'd lived in Ireland for nearly three hundred years—knew the texture of its ground, the scent of its air, every hill and valley, river and pond. The air had a briny tang to it— they were near the sea.

When his eyes adjusted to the misty dark, moonlight penetrating through tatters in the low-hanging clouds, he saw a ruin on a rise to his left. Stark stone ended in a jagged parapet that had been destroyed centuries ago in some forgotten battle.

"Shite," he whispered.

Why had his dream, vision, astral projection, whatever the hell it was, brought him *here*?

He started for the hill topped by the ruined castle. Ben, without question, followed, his footsteps silent, his presence palpable.

As Dylan neared the ruin, he saw lights. Not firelight but the harsh glare of electric lanterns, headlights, the laser gleams of scopes.

No ...

Dylan began to run. Ben, behind him, breathed hard. "Hey, slow down," Ben called. "I'm pushing a thousand and fifteen. Not as young as I used to be."

Dylan wasn't either, but he might have been a cub just past his Transition for the energy that boosted him up the hill. He sprinted the last few hundred feet and halted abruptly, seeing ... himself.

A black-maned lion growled ferociously at a ring of soldiers and police that surrounded him and four other figures. The lion lunged, only to be halted by a shock stick that sent him to his belly, but he didn't cease his ground-vibrating snarls.

One of the soldiers had a younger man in a choke-hold, a gun pressed to his forehead. The lad, who looked much like Dylan—blue eyes, midnight hair—was Dylan's youngest son, Kenny, whom Sean's cub had been named for. Kenny struggled and cursed, spitting blood, desperately trying to reach the soldier who held a terrified but snarling young woman. Her belly was swollen in obvious pregnancy, very near her delivery.

Dylan raced forward, but Ben's strong hand yanked him back. "You can't interfere."

Dylan rounded on him, letting his shift come. His claws elongated and tore at Ben's hand.

"Ow!" Ben jerked away. "Chillax, Dylan. You can't do anything. I mean, you *can't* interact. We're not really here."

"Why?" Dylan demanded in a fierce growl. "Why are you showing me this?"

"Showing you what?" Ben asked, as though he didn't know.

"The night my sons and I were captured. It was Yule, twenty-five years ago."

"Christmas past," Ben muttered.

"What?"

"Nothing."

"They rounded us up. They tried to separate us,

tried to take Sinead, Kenny's mate. She was about to have Connor."

Under the blare of lights, Liam broke free of those holding him and went for the man with Sinead, who was snarling and fighting with strength of her own. Her terror streamed from her and touched Dylan—she was afraid the soldiers would take her cub, rip it from her to do experiments as rumor had told them had happened to others.

Shock sticks struck Liam, but only slowed him a little. He lunged for Sinead, closing his hands around her just as a rope landed around Liam's neck and yanked him back. Liam, choking, scrabbled at the noose with one hand while he kept tight hold of Sinead with the other.

Then Sean was there. The Sword of the Guardian gleamed in his hand, and he struck, silently and swiftly. His sword sliced the rope that bound Liam, deflected an arm that raised a shock stick, batted aside another man with a tranq rifle.

Even in his fury, Sean wouldn't take a human life. The Sword of the Guardian wasn't meant for that, though it could be a deadly weapon.

"Stop him!" a soldier shouted in a no-nonsense London accent. "Take him down!"

Sean leapt, shifting as he went, his clothes ripping

away, until a lion soared over the soldiers' heads. Two tranq rifles went off. Sean buckled in mid-air and fell in a groaning tangle on the ground, the Sword of the Guardian landing beside him. A policeman, one of the Irish Garda, picked it up, then dropped it as though it burned.

Sean's attack had taken attention away from Liam and Dylan. Liam slipped off into the darkness with Sinead, the two disappearing as only Shifters could. Dylan sprang from his low crouch at the men who still held Kenny.

He'd had to calculate it just right, to separate the man with the gun from Kenny before the gun went off. Fortunately, Kenny, a wily Morrissey Feline, knew what to do. He dropped straight down, taking the man's legs out with him. While the soldiers and Dylan tangled together, Kenny escaped in a flat-out run, sprinting into darkness after Liam and his mate.

It took eight soldiers to subdue Dylan. He was on a wild rampage, teeth and claws, though Dylan wouldn't kill, even then. Shifters weren't murderers.

Watching from the base of the damp hill with Ben, Dylan regretted that choice. If he'd killed all the soldiers and police—thirty men had come to round up the Morrissey family—and taken his sons to the still-wild places in Eastern Europe or a remote area of South America, they'd have survived. They'd even now be without Collars, without captivity, without playing into the hands of their greatest enemies. And Kenny and Sinead might still be alive.

The men finally conquered Dylan, not with tranqs or shock sticks, but by lifting Sean's limp form from the ground. Sean, unconscious, had shifted back to human, his naked body bruised from the tranq darts, burned from the shocks.

"He attacked to kill," the soldier who'd commanded them to take down Sean said to the lion. "We're authorized to execute him right here."

Dylan roared. He tried to shake the men off him— ten of them now, but only got shocked for his troubles.

He quickly shifted to human. A few soldiers backed off, but the rest surrounded him, one with an arm around Dylan's neck, ready to break it. These men were well-trained and skilled fighters, likely hand-picked for this mission.

"Leave Sean be," Dylan choked out. "He won't hurt you."

"He came at us with a weapon. That's grounds for instant termination."

Dylan dragged in breaths, lion's growls in his chest. "Please." Dylan never pled, never begged for mercy. "Don't take my son."

Dylan had lost his mate, mother to his three boys. He couldn't stand any more loss, and not his precious sons, Sinead, his unborn grandson.

The British soldier came to stand in front of Dylan. He had a scarred face, a shaved head, and hard eyes. A man who'd seen much, probably had fought in difficult places all his life.

"Then call in the ones who ran off. They come with us, and you all live. Otherwise, we terminate this one, and then you."

Dylan didn't care so much for his own life. He'd already lived a long time, had seen too much, like this soldier he faced. But he knew damn well they'd kill Sean, then they'd hunt Liam and Kenny until they caught and murdered them. What they'd do to Sinead and her cub, he didn't even want to know.

"Give me your promise," Dylan said. "Your word that they'll live, that my grandchild won't be taken to one of your filthy labs and dissected."

The man didn't blink. "Shifters are being put into communities in the United States, not dissected."

"The fuck they're not."

The look in the soldier's eyes told Dylan he was right. The soldier didn't like the job he'd been given to do, but he'd do it because it was his duty, and he didn't disobey orders.

"Give me your word," Dylan repeated. A man like this would abide by his promise, he sensed, even to an enemy.

"I'll take you to a holding facility. Alive. But only if the others come in and surrender."

"Sinead stays with us," Dylan said firmly.

The man's mouth flattened, but finally, he gave Dylan a nod. "The woman stays with you."

Dylan took a step back. The men holding him tensed, but the soldier gave them a gesture to let Dylan go.

Down the hill, the present-day Dylan watched, sick at heart, as his old self shifted back to lion and began to roar.

It was the endless, barking roar that a lion sent over his territory, warning every beast to crawl away or face the consequences. It was the roar that told his family to come to him.

The roar also held grief, a knowledge that he was betraying his sons and giving up their freedom. The sound rose to the misty sky, full of mourning and defeat.

This was the first of many, many terrible decisions Dylan had been forced to make on the road to Shifter-town, but this one had been hardest of all, and he'd never truly recovered from it. To save Sean, he'd sent them all to captivity.

The lion's roar shook the earth. Mist swirled into opaque threads between Dylan and Ben, obscuring the tableau on the hill.

Dylan knew what happened next—Liam and Kenny returned with Sinead, and all of them were locked in spelled chains and taken to a detention facility, where the Collars were put on them.

Dylan shuddered, praying to the Goddess that he wouldn't have to watch the pain and horror of their first contact with the Collars. Sinead had never regained her strength after that, dying when she brought Connor into the world at the end of their long journey from Ireland to Texas.

The Goddess must have taken pity on Dylan, because the mist grew thicker, colder, and blotted out the scene. Dylan felt his feet lift from the ground before he tumbled into blackness, his only contact in the dark the tight grip of Ben's hand.

When his vision cleared, Dylan again lay under the rubble in the bedroom in the haunted house, stiff, unmoving, once more unable to breathe.

Ben was gone. A different pair of hands moved a beam crushing Dylan's legs, and sunlight stabbed painfully into Dylan's unblinking eyes.

Silhouetted against the light was a broad-shouldered man with stark white hair, two locks of which fell forward in long braids glinting with beads. Dylan wished he could groan.

"Dylan!" Zander Moncrieff boomed in his huge polar-bear voice. "You do not look good, my friend."

CHAPTER THREE

Though Zander could be an irritating smart-ass, Dylan sent up thanks to the Goddess for sending him.

He was a polar bear, un-Collared, who'd lived among humans most of his life, and right now, exactly who Dylan needed. Zander was that rarest of creatures —a Shifter healer.

"How did you know?" Dylan's voice again sounded without his lips moving or any breath coming past them.

"Know what? That you're buried in two-hundred-year old beams? No idea, actually." Zander's black eyes glittered. "I'm here because it's my turn."

Dylan growled. "What gobshite are you talking now?"

"Wow, having a ceiling fall on you makes you cranky."

"I apologize." Dylan gritted his teeth—or at least gritted them mentally. "I know the healing will hurt, but I'm ready."

"Healing?" Zander looked surprised. "Oh, I'm not here to heal you, old friend."

Dylan wished he could close his eyes. He knew he was dying, but he wasn't ready. Much too much to do first. He wanted to watch his grandchildren grow up—take their first steps, learn to be Shifters, move through their Transitions, fall in love and form the mate bond. He wanted them to be Collarless, out of Shiftertowns, free.

"Did Rae come with you?" Dylan named Zander's mate, who was the only female Guardian. "If she doesn't mind, I'd prefer Sean to do it. If he can."

"Send you to dust, you mean?"

The Sword of the Guardian had been forged to separate a Shifter's soul from his or her body at death. The soul was free to enter the Summerland, safe from capture, while the body vanished as dust.

Zander rubbed his chin. "Sean's a little busy right now. Yule celebration and all."

Of course he was. Dylan didn't want to pull Sean from his happiness, didn't want to turn Yule into a Morrissey tragedy. "Rae, then. If she's all right with it."

Zander shook his head, the white braids moving. "Rae's not here. She's home, waiting for her dad to light the Yule log. She's carrying my cub—did you know? Makes her growly and not as hot to travel. But so beautiful." He beamed with pride.

"Then fetch Kendrick. Please."

Kendrick was another Guardian, and the leader of a group of un-Collared Shifters. Dylan had worked closely with him this past year and had come to call him friend.

"He's busy too. Do you really think anyone's free for you today? Yule's one of the biggest celebrations of the year. And now that we've adopted a lot of human customs, we're all busy, busy. Last minute shopping, baking the fruitcake ... Hey, you have any idea exactly what's in fruitcake? Why would you put fruit in a cake? In a *pie*, now, that I understand—"

"Zander what the fuck are you doing here?" Sometimes the only way to stop Zander was to bludgeon through his speech. "Did you come to talk me to death?"

"What? No, no." Zander chuckled. "You're not going to die, my friend. Well ... maybe you won't. Or maybe you will."

"Send Ben back up here. He at least makes some sense."

"Ben?" Zander gave him a puzzled look. "Haven't

seen Ben at all. House is empty. Except for you, that is. And, you know, the house."

Where the hell was Ben then? He'd agreed to be backup at the meeting tonight—if this was indeed the morning after Dylan had arrived. It wasn't like Ben to miss an appointment.

Dylan subsided, reluctantly realizing he had no control over the situation. He hated not having control, but here he was, immobilized and near death, while Zander, the only Shifter on earth who could save his life, mused about holiday desserts.

"Tell you what," Zander said. "I'm going to show you why everyone's so busy, and no one has time to send you to dust. Not that they'd want to. They need you."

"I can't do them much good lying here not breathing."

"You have a point. Now, I'm taking your hand ... there we go. No bones broken in it—that's good. Healing hand bones is a bitch."

As Zander spoke, the room began to spin. Zander's strong grip jerked Dylan from the rubble with a force that made Dylan want to scream.

Darkness swallowed them, wind rushing like the last time, but the air wasn't as cold. It felt damp, but held the dampness of the southern United States instead of the Irish coast.

The humidity died as they rolled and tumbled through the blackness, Dylan's only anchor Zander's giant and overly strong hand. He heard the growl of a polar bear, which was comforting. As grating as Zander's constant buoyancy could be, he was large, formidable, fearless, and one hell of a fighter. Plus, though Dylan would never admit it out loud, his fur was soft.

Dylan slammed to a halt, face down on the earth. Zander grunted as he landed in a heap next to him then climbed stiffly to his feet.

Once more, Dylan could move. He could draw a breath, blink, grip Zander's hand to rise and steady himself.

To Dylan's surprise, they stood in his own back-yard. The house he lived in with Glory, Sean and family, and Liam's house next door, opened to a long strip of grass and trees that ran behind the bungalows.

The Shifters held most of their celebrations in this common area. Liam and Kim, Sean and Andrea, and many others had mated here under sun and moon. Dylan had performed the ceremonies in the first years in Shiftertown, and now Liam had taken over his role.

They also held memorials here—sadly too many of those—burning offerings to the Goddess for the soul of the departed. Every Yule, every spring equinox, summer solstice, Mabon, Samhain, and festivals in between, the Shifters gathered to give thanks to the Goddess. Then they partied.

When humans had hammered out the agreements that put Shifters into Shiftertowns, one thing the humans had conceded was to allow the Shifters to maintain their religious festivals. A few humans on the committee were adamant about the freedom of religion clause in the First Amendment, though others were quick to point out that many Shifters came from lands outside the United States. No matter—the Shifters won that point. They were allowed their Goddess festivals.

The unlit Yule log was already in place in a cleared-out area, well away from the houses. Cubs played around it, tying ribbons, streamers, and other decorations to the log, which would be set alight after dark.

Which would be soon. The sky was already dimming, the sun going down, though Dylan swore the trip from New Orleans had taken only a few minutes.

Spell. The only explanation for this weirdness was some kind of magic that made time immaterial.

Either that or Dylan was having one hell of a dream. But if he were dreaming, wouldn't he conjure someone less irritating to take him on these journeys than Zander or Ben? Why not Glory? Or his granddaughter, Katriona, who was growing so fast, or his smiling daughter-in-law, Kim? Dylan would far prefer to spend his last delirious moments with one of them.

Katriona herself came bounding out of Liam's house. She was nearly three, and had the strength and energy of a lion cub. A white-haired lad, the orphaned Olaf, ran after her, followed by a brown bear cub, another orphan called Katie, whom eleven-year-old Olaf felt responsible for. He liked to take care of cubs.

"Katriona," Dylan called to her. "Come give your old grandad a hug."

Katriona ignored him and kept running, ribbons in her hand. Olaf overtook her, grabbing the ribbons before they could trip her. Katie gamboled around them, trying to snatch the ribbons with her mouth.

Dylan let out a sigh. "Don't tell me. She can't hear me."

"Nope." Zander looked around. "Too bad. This looks like one hell of a party."

"Shouldn't you be at your own Yule gathering? In Montana? With your mate?"

Zander continued to watch the Shifters, the crowd growing as the sun went down. There was Ronan and his human mate, Elizabeth, her slightly delinquent sister, Mabel, who held Ronan's cub, still a baby. With them were Rebecca and Walker. Rebecca, a Kodiak bear Shifter, was pregnant with Walker's cub. Carrying a cub didn't make Rebecca growly—she was happier than Dylan had ever seen her. It did make her loud, her laughter echoing up and down the clearing.

Spike and Myka, Ellison and Maria, Broderick and Joanna, Mason and Jasmine, Deni and Jace, Tiger and Carly ... and more couples who'd formed in the years since this Shiftertown began, spilled around the Yule log. All there, plus plenty of cubs, including Tiger's daughter, who stuck close to Connor, and Shifters who were hoping to mate soon.

Kendrick's crew would show up well after dark. They'd hold their own celebration at their compound south and west of Austin, then slip in and join the friends they'd made in this Shiftertown.

Darkness came quickly. A roar rose from the gathering crowd as Liam, as Shiftertown leader, gave thanks to the Goddess and touched the first flame to the Yule log.

The Shifters watched the small flame flicker, then they surged forward to light more branches, keeping the cubs well back ... or at least trying to. The cubs cheered, and the adult Shifters took up their cries. Some stripped off clothes and shifted, and soon snarls, howls, roars, and growls joined the human voices.

Liam scooped Kim into his arms and kissed her. The kiss turned passionate, and those around them laughed and whooped. The Shifters would be seeking kisses and more as the night wore on.

Dylan's heart warmed through his worry. Liam had found happiness, as had Sean, in ways neither brother had dreamed.

"What is this meant to show me?" Dylan asked Zander. "That my family can enjoy themselves without me? I already knew that."

"Nope. To show you how far they've come."

Dylan looked again. There were more cubs scampering about this year than ever. Shifters were healthier, better-fed, females were having more cubs and not dying of bringing them in. Everywhere he saw Shifter families hugging, playing, celebrating.

"If you're trying to tell me captivity is a good thing ..."

"Hell no." Zander scowled. "You see *me* grabbing a Collar and locking it around my neck? Only reason I live in a Shiftertown is because my sweetie is its Guardian, plus she doesn't want to stray far from her family." He swept his hand toward the collected Shifters. "Those tough decisions we made in the beginning—they're paying off. We're stronger, ready to fight. If we'd fought the humans before, we never would have made it. Now, we'll be able to stand up and demand things—we've already started to. And fight off the Fae, of course. Can't forget about those slime balls."

"*I* remember making hard decisions, lad." Putting Connor into a Collar had torn Dylan apart inside. "Which ones did you make?"

Zander slanted him a sideways glance. "You don't want to know, my friend. You do not want to know."

Dylan let that go. Zander was enigmatic about his deep past, to everyone but Rae.

"Anyway," Zander went on. "Yeah, I *am* showing you that your family has a fine time without you. If you keep missing their parties, they're going to forget to ask you to them. It's a lesson I'm supposed to be teaching you." He spread his arms in a grandiose gesture and addressed the sky. "I am the spirit of Christmas Presents." He lowered his hands. "Wait—why do Christmas gifts need a spirit? Unless they're *magical* presents ..."

"You mean the Spirit of Christmas Present," Dylan said dryly. "I read that story when it was first published. I'm no Ebenezer Scrooge."

"Sure, you're not." Zander gave him a skeptical look. "Which is why you're hunkering by yourself in a dark and empty house while your family is dancing, drinking, feasting ..."

"I didn't go there to avoid my family, and you know it. I'm making another hard decision ..."

Tiger, a very large man with orange-and-black

striped hair, halted right in front of them. He cradled his cub, Seth, against his chest with one large hand.

Zander waved. "Hey, big guy."

Tiger studied the air in front of him, frowning as though he thought he saw something but wasn't sure. He stood for a long time, sniffing delicately, testing for scent.

His son gurgled, and Tiger's attention snapped back to him. Tiger walked away, heading for Carly. He threw one puzzled glance over his shoulder then focused on Carly, sliding his arm around her and sinking into her embrace.

"He senses what's real," Zander said. "Even if others can't. Tiger's a strange and wonderful Shifter."

Dylan wasn't listening. Another strange and wonderful Shifter had caught his gaze—Glory, dressed in red leather with a white, sparkly sweater that glittered like snow in moonlight.

She was swaying to music pumping out from speakers Sean had set up, dancing *very* close to a Feline—a leopard from an arrogant family who thought they were the next hot things in Shiftertown. The Feline was in human form, in jeans and a leather jacket, sliding his knee between Glory's as they gyrated together. Glory had a wide smile on her face, and placed her hand on the Feline's shoulder.

"Excuse me," Dylan said tightly.

He strode across the clearing, making his way toward Glory, ignoring Zander's, "Nothing you can do about it. You're not really here ..."

Dylan reached Glory and yanked her away from the son of a bitch.

CHAPTER FOUR

———————

At least, Dylan *tried* to yank her away. His hands went right through Glory, as insubstantial as smoke.

The dance continued. Dylan could smell the Feline, the wood smoke in his clothes, the whisky on his breath.

"Glory," Dylan yelled into her ear, over the music. "Lass."

She didn't hear him. Glory was six feet tall with the curves to match, a Lupine with a wolf's grace and gray-eyed stare. At the moment, her eyes were half closed, her body catching the beat of the music.

Dylan reached for her, but again, his hand connected with nothing.

He gathered his strength. Dylan had never allowed anything or anyone to get the better of him, or to stand between himself and something he truly wanted. He saw, he acted.

He concentrated on every cell in his body, willing them to obey. Then he wrapped himself around Glory.

He was still incorporeal from her perspective, but he slid like water over her body, pressing every part of her.

Glory jumped. She glared at the Feline dancing with her, her eyes changing to the white-gray of a wolf, a snarl snapping from her throat. She shoved the Feline away. "What the fuck?"

He blinked at her in startled confusion. "What?"

"I'm mated, asshole. Or as good as. Can't we just enjoy a dance?"

"What the hell are you talking about?" The Feline stopped dancing and held up his hands. "I haven't touched you."

"Sure, dick-brain. Go paw at someone else."

The Feline wrinkled his nose in a parody of a leopard snarl. "What I get for going after Dylan's leavings."

Glory sprang at him, her Collar sparking. Dylan tangled himself in her, slowing her down, and her eyes widened.

So did the eyes of the Feline. Glory in attack mode wasn't something to mess with. The Feline turned around and hurried off.

The sparks on Glory's Collar abruptly died. "Who's touching me?" She inhaled, reading scent. "Dylan ...? Where are you?" She swung around, head turning as she searched the space around her.

"Here, love." Dylan caressed her with his misty body. He cupped her breasts, dipped his hand between her legs.

"Oh." Glory's voice softened, her skin warming under his touch. "Wow. Either I drank too much or I'm having one hell of a fantasy."

"I'm with you." Dylan whispered into her ear, then licked her earlobe. "Come inside with me."

"Holy Goddess," she whispered, her limbs going slack.

Dylan felt her heart beating faster, her breath increasing, her desires rising. He kissed her, barely able to feel her lips, but he willed himself to solidify until she kissed him back.

"Dylan," she whispered. "I don't know how you're doing this, but ... I *like* it."

"In the house," Dylan said.

Glory headed that direction. Others called to her, suggesting she come dance, join a circle around the Yule log, have some of these fantastic burgers, but she only waved and kept walking.

Small Kenny, looking over Andrea's shoulder as Glory went past her, fixed his gray gaze directly on

Dylan. Those keen eyes sharpened, meeting Dylan's without trouble.

"Gan-Da," he declared.

"No, sweetheart," Andrea said, jouncing him. "Your Grandda's not here. He said he'll be back tomorrow."

Kenny didn't answer. He kept his serious eyes on Dylan as Dylan led Glory up the porch stairs into the empty house.

———

GLORY DIDN'T KNOW WHAT CRAZY DREAM THIS was, but it was amazing. She swore she heard Dylan's voice, felt his touch—no one knew how to touch her like Dylan.

"Easy, lass," she heard his whisper as she reached the bedroom. "Don't give way too soon."

Glory wanted to explode. She pulled off her clothes and lay on top of the bed—even if this was just a dream, she could enjoy it.

But it was so real. Glory sensed Dylan around her, cradling her, loving her, but she couldn't see him. She couldn't truly *feel* him, not like having him next to her in the flesh, but then again, his presence was palpable.

His hands touched her thighs, his hot breath too, and then came the sensation of his fingers, his tongue, bringing her to life. She wanted to hold him, caress him —and also wanted to grab his quite substantial cock and delight in it. Frustrated, she reached for him, but he remained elusive.

What Dylan did to her wasn't elusive. Need built inside her, Dylan's fingers doing their magic, his tongue and mouth providing a hot and skilled assist.

Glory stopped struggling to touch him and lay back to bask in his thorough attention. She gripped the covers of the bed they shared, arching into the mattress.

The cool air on her body caressed her like a lover. Or maybe that was Dylan. Lacy shadows danced across the ceiling, Glory fixing on them as her body heated beyond the bearable.

Growls tore from her throat, the she-wolf not far below her surface. It wanted to emerge, needed to.

Sometimes she and Dylan drove far into the countryside, seeking a remote stream or woods a long way from any town. There, they shifted to their animal forms and went at it with all the ferocity they had to tamp down when they were human-shaped.

If Glory shifted now, would Dylan shift as well? Taking her in wildness?

Just the idea made her release want to come. Dimly she realized that if she did shift, and Andrea came to check on her, Andrea would see Glory in wolf form writhing and squealing alone on the bed. She suppressed the need, but it wasn't easy.

"Dylan," she groaned. "I'm sorry. Whatever you're torturing me for I'm ... No, wait." Her breath came too fast, her words slurring. "I'm not sorry. I'll do it again. And again. And ... Oh, dear Goddess ..."

She was coming. Glory reached for Dylan, found nothing, and seized a pillow instead. She bunched it so hard in her fists that it ripped, feathers bursting upward.

The pillow was torn from her hands, and Dylan was there. Sort of. She saw his outline, his burning blue eyes, felt his weight on her.

Glory came apart as he pushed inside her, nothing vague about his large cock now. She didn't muffle her cries as he began to thrust—the revelry outside drowned out the sound.

She shouted his name, heard, "Lass," in his beautiful whisper in her ear.

I love you, came her shaky thought.

Hot awareness took over. She wrapped her arms around Dylan, rewarded with the firmness of his back, the fierceness of his mouth on hers.

They came together, he growling her name in that faint but rumbling tone. Dylan didn't hold back—he never did with her, knowing Glory was strong enough to take him.

Glory was breathless by the time she felt Dylan's touch on her face, his final, "Lass." And suddenly he was gone.

The warmth of him vanished, and his whisper died. A cool rush of air stirred the curtains at the window then ... nothing.

Glory gathered the remains of the pillow and held it tightly, tears spilling from her eyes. Her sobs turned to the howls of a wolf, lonely and mournful against the music and laughter that pounded in the crystal air outside.

———

"THERE YOU ARE," ZANDER SAID WHEN DYLAN returned to him. Zander had a beer in his hand. "All done?"

Dylan resisted the urge to straighten his clothes. His jeans and jacket were perfectly in place, because what he'd done with Glory hadn't really happened.

Or had it? This in-between thing was maddening.

Holding Glory had been real, he was certain of it. Her heat, her scent, her voice, her beauty—all her. Dylan's mind couldn't have conjured out of nothing the true Glory and her enjoyment of lovemaking. She was amazing.

"Done for now," Dylan answered.

Zander had raised his beer to take a sip, but he burst out laughing. "You have it bad, my friend. When are the sun and moon ceremonies? Any mate bond happening?"

"Not really your business." His answer was curt because the question had been on Dylan's mind, and he knew it was on Glory's.

But first things first. He couldn't be distracted by mate issues while he was trying to save Shifters from extinction. Once Shifters were safe, free, and living in peace, he and Glory could have a long discussion about their future.

Dylan knew damn well life wasn't so tidy, but grief and fighting for the lives of others had taken its toll on him. Hence, he'd gone to New Orleans to meet with dangerous beings so the Shifters dancing like maniacs around the glowing Yule log could keep enjoying themselves.

Zander set his beer on a tree stump, sighing with regret. "Time to go."

"Already?" Dylan watched Andrea and Sean swaying together, Kenny perched on Sean's shoulders. Dylan wanted to stay and soak up the warmth of his family—he'd already sacrificed too much of that.

Zander shrugged. "I don't make the rules."

"Who does?" Dylan pinned him with a stare. "Who is doing this to me?"

"I have no idea. The thing is—am *I* really doing this? Or are you just projecting me?"

Dylan regarded him calmly. "If I were to conjure a guide to the spirit world, I doubt I'd conjure you."

"Good point. Well, anyway ..."

Zander waved at the crowd, as though they could see him. Then he caught Dylan's hand with fingers like a coil of constrictors ready for their next meal.

The warmth, light, laughter, and love ripped away like running watercolors. Dizziness smacked Dylan, and darkness tumbled him and Zander end over end, as the wind whipped around them, the cold now biting.

When light returned, Dylan was back in the room in New Orleans, again buried in debris, feeling no pain but unable even to twitch.

Zander had vanished, and a last beam of afternoon sunlight pierced the room. But was this the same day? The next day? The next week? The fact that Dylan was still aware must mean that not a lot of time had passed, else he'd be dead.

Perhaps he already was. Perhaps his soul drifted from place to place, experiencing the past, the present. Why he'd see Ben and Zander, he did not know, but they were both highly magical beings. Maybe some part of them responded to his lost and drifting soul.

Depressing. Dylan did not want to be dead, not now, and worse, his soul did not need to be floating around, ripe pickings for any Fae who sensed it. Fae were nasty enough to living Shifters they enslaved—Shifter souls fared even worse. A live Shifter at least could die, be sent to dust, and so be free of them. A soul could be trapped forever. Dylan hoped Zander would bring a Guardian soon.

A scraping sound cut off his thoughts. Dylan was already as still as he could be, but he focused, wondering who came for him now.

Someone was climbing stairs, someone who moved with a strange gait, dragging its way to the top. At the landing, it paused, then came on. Dylan heard its grating breaths, its slow but steady progress down the hall.

The being reached the doorway. Paused. Then moved forward toward the pile under which Dylan was partially buried.

A misshapen hand, this one more skeletal than Ben's massive one, grasped a beam and hauled it aside with great strength.

Dylan looked up at a hooded form—not a cowled robe, but a man in a hoodie, his eyes glaring red in a skull-like face.

Dylan relaxed a fraction. "Apologies if I am late for our meeting," he tried to say. "Slight delay."

This time, nothing emerged. The words rang inside Dylan's head but didn't sound in the room.

The man growled. He stank of death, and when his skeletal fingers touched Dylan, the cold of them burned past Dylan's paralyzed state.

They were blood drinkers. Bitter enemies of the Fae. Enemies of anyone, really, but they had promised to speak to Dylan about an alliance. It had to be on the solstice, they said, and then only. This was the shortest day and longest night in the northern hemisphere, when the *zilithal* could most easily gather.

Did Dylan trust them? Not at all. But he'd rather have them on the Shifter side than lurking to ambush them after Shifters had defeated the Fae.

The bloodsucker came closer. Dylan again tried to speak, to make his thoughts heard as he had with Ben and Zander. Nothing.

Likely this *zilithal* had been sent to see if Dylan was on his way. Finding him trapped, mostly dead and unable to fight, must seem serendipitous. *Free meal*.

Why the haunted house had allowed the creature inside, Dylan couldn't say. Sometimes it let in unlikely people, but it was not kind to evil beings, or even anyone who tried to hurt the house's inhabitants. He remembered how Mason, who'd mated with the house's owner, gleefully told the story of the house walling up Jasmine's obnoxious boyfriend.

The house had also murdered a Fae who had charged into it, ready to kill the Shifters Jaycee and

Dimitri, who'd been staying here while they fulfilled a mission of their own.

"I hope you choke on me," was Dylan's last thought before the *zilithal* pulled back his hood, seized Dylan, and sank his teeth into the curve of Dylan's neck.

There was a crash, followed by a growl like the rumble of thunder. A massive Shifter grabbed the bloodsucker, hauled it off Dylan, and twisted the *zilithal* until it was a mass of unmoving, dead bones.

CHAPTER FIVE

————————

Dylan breathed out in relief, or at least would if he could. "Tiger."

Tiger dropped the last of the dry bones and gazed at Dylan with his yellow eyes. Those eyes hid a swiftly calculating brain but also a gentle soul who loved with astonishing fury.

"You should not be here," Tiger announced.

"That idea is occurring to me, lad."

"You should not be here at all."

"And if you help me up and get Zander back here to heal me, I'll take your advice."

Tiger frowned, as though deciding how to respond. Sometimes he didn't speak at all, keeping his quickly moving thoughts silent. Other times Dylan heard his rumbling voice going on at length to Carly, telling her stories or talking about whatever they found to converse on. Carly would laugh, her happiness vivid.

"You coming here unmade everything," Tiger said after a time.

"What are you talking about?" Dylan demanded. "The bloodsuckers? They have information on the Fae I can find nowhere else."

"Best to leave them be. They can't be trusted."

"I didn't say I would *trust* them. I've been trying to speak to the *zilithal* for a year. Finally, I convinced a few to meet with me."

"Alone."

"With Ben," Dylan said impatiently. "I'm not foolish enough to go in without backup. I'd have asked you along, but it's the Yule festival. The rest of you deserve a day off, and I didn't want to get into it with Carly." She was a sweet woman but wasn't afraid to tell Dylan to cease dragging Tiger into dangerous situations.

Tiger nudged the bones, which were beginning to disintegrate. "They understand only one thing. Death."

"How do you know?" Dylan asked. "No one knew about these creatures until recently. I learned of their existence only a year ago."

"Now, many people know of them. You unleashed them."

Dylan growled. "Stop talking rubbish, lad, and get me out of here."

Tiger reached down and gripped Dylan's arms. Unlike when Ben or Zander grabbed his hand, this hurt. Dylan spent some time swearing while Tiger propped him on his feet.

"Well," Dylan said, realizing he could breathe again. "Are we going?"

The world didn't spin this time. Tiger lifted Dylan over his shoulder, stepped across the rubble, and carried him from the room.

They were outside in the blink of an eye. The world felt different, with a pall in it Dylan couldn't place.

The next thing Dylan knew, he was on the back of Tiger's motorcycle, Tiger in front of him. Pain Dylan had never experienced rattled him as Tiger started up and glided down the drive to the road.

"Where's Ben?" Dylan asked him.

"Dead," Tiger said, and then nothing could be heard over the roar of the bike.

———

DYLAN DIDN'T REMEMBER TIME PASSING, BUT THE sun was setting as they reached Shiftertown in Austin. Or where Shiftertown should be.

The old airport, Mueller, had gradually been gentrified with offices and swanky new apartments, but the development seemed to have tripled overnight. Dylan saw no empty lots as Tiger zipped past.

Shiftertown lay in a hollow to the north and west of Mueller, a pocket of bungalows left over from the early twentieth century.

As soon as Tiger rounded the corner by the bar Liam managed and through the open gates, Dylan noticed the silence. The setting sun glared in his eyes and when the beam finally dipped below the trees, Tiger stopped the bike. Dylan, who could move again, staggered from it.

The bungalows were gone. Foundations and partial walls remained here and there, but the houses had been gutted. The occasional gaping hole showed where a Shifter family's secret space had lain, where they'd gathered those things most valuable to them.

"What the fuck?" Dylan demanded.

He heard the steady *beep, beep, beep* of a backup indicator from heavy machinery. A flash of yellow caught his eye, and he saw a bulldozer plowing away the remnants of a house down the street—Spike's he thought.

The home Dylan shared with Glory, Sean, and Andrea was gone, as was Liam and Kim's house. Across the street, Ellison Rowe's bungalow was half fallen in, derelict. There was a dank tang in the air, and the stench of decay.

Dylan rounded on Tiger in panic. "Where is Glory? My family? The cubs? They were just here."

He dashed into what had been the common area, where Shifters had danced, chased each other, gorged themselves, and enjoyed being alive. In the middle, where the Yule log had burned, was a large pile of black ash, cold and stirring in the wind.

Tiger was suddenly next to him. "Gone," he said in a monotone. "A few years ago now. The Fae came through the ley line. And Shifters died."

"What?" Dylan fought to keep calm. "Tell me what the hell you mean. A few *years* ago?"

Tiger nodded. "To you, it is something to come. But I witnessed it."

"Fuck." Dylan turned in a circle, searching for any homes he recognized, but none were left standing. The bulldozer was steadily clearing—making way for more new development now that the Shifters were gone.

"*What* Shifters died?" Dylan asked. "My sons?" Tiger's nod destroyed something inside him. "Grand-children?" he continued fearfully.

"Connor got away. And my daughter. They took as many cubs as they could. I hid them."

Some relief in the horror, but not much. "Glory?"

"She died like a warrior, killing many Fae before they took her down.'"

The grief of that struck him like a sledgehammer. Dylan's face grew wet with silent tears.

"What the hell happened? The Fae came through the ley line? What about Andrea's father? He's supposed to be protecting the gate from his side." Andrea's father, a Fae, guarded the Shifters because of her.

Tiger shrugged. "The Fae fight many wars among themselves. He lost."

"Son of a bitch." Dylan dragged in a breath, trying to *think*. "He was one of their most powerful generals. I counted on him."

"You were not here," Tiger said. "You could not provide him what he needed in time."

"What do you mean, I wasn't here? Where the hell was I? Killed in the haunted house? None of this makes any sense ..." Dylan scrubbed his hair. "Wait. Are you showing me what actually will happen? Or what *might* happen?"

"Your decision to meet the *zilithal* in New Orleans on the solstice kicked off a string of events. Beginning with the death of Ben and yourself."

The *zilithal*, the bloodsuckers. Not exactly vampires, which were humans turned into drinkers of blood, but creatures born of a dark world, who'd worked their way into the Fae realm. They'd fought the Fae hard and killed many before the Fae finally expelled them. They were trying to survive in the human world now ...

"Not survive," Dylan said slowly. "They want to take over." He looked at Tiger who regarded him passively, probably knowing this already. "They want to take this world, like they tried to with Faerie. Their greatest natural enemy here are the Shifters."

"And you are the strongest of the Shifter leaders," Tiger finished.

Dylan clapped his hands on top of his head and swore for a time in Gaelic. "Fuck!" he shouted. "Fuck them, and fuck my arrogant shit of a brain. I thought I was so clever setting up a meet to get them to spill everything they knew about besting the Fae. They *played* me."

Tiger nodded solemnly. "Played you well."

"We have to stop it." Dylan ceased his wild pacing and headed for the motorcycle. "We have to get me out of New Orleans, and Ben too. Wake me up, snap me out of the paralysis, find me a healer—something."

Tiger came behind him, pushing Dylan out of the way so he could mount and start his motorcycle. "It has already happened."

"Don't tell me that. We have to do *something*. You're a walking genius, Tiger. Figure it out."

Tiger turned his head to stare at him with his enigmatic golden eyes, but didn't argue.

"Tiger." Dylan gentled his voice. "Carly?"

Tiger's eyes warmed. "She is safe." His voice rang with strength and confidence.

"Good," Dylan said, but his word was drowned when Tiger started the bike and tore out of Shiftertown.

————

TIGER TOOK THEM WITH UNERRING EASE TO THE warehouse area in New Orleans where Dylan and Ben were to meet with the *zilithal*. The place was eerily quiet, which was why Dylan had chosen it.

He'd scheduled the meeting to start an hour after dark. Dylan was too disoriented to know what time it was, or even what day it was, as he and Tiger rolled through the streets, but he saw shadows slipping around the deserted buildings. Tiger killed the bike and shut off the light, but he didn't seem worried about being seen—they were still in the *not-there* state.

Tiger led the way to the door of the warehouse Dylan had chosen for the meeting. Dylan had scouted the location carefully for weeks, asking Ben to help with that. This building had long been abandoned and was half falling down—whoever owned the property had no interest in keeping it up. Or maybe the property had been foreclosed on, and no enterprising person had wanted to buy it from whatever bank or mortgage company had repossessed it—didn't matter.

No one ever came this way. The outer warehouses were in use but this place was avoided even by gangs who roamed the territory. It was reputed to be haunted, Ben had told him. Perfect for Dylan's purpose.

Dylan caught sight of a bloodsucker in the shadows —he'd never have seen it if he weren't Shifter. Tiger ignored it to wrench open the battered metal door.

The noise of fighting came to them over the squeal of the hinges. Dylan heard roaring that was familiar, along with the powerful voice of Ben, shouting words he only used when he was *truly* pissed off.

Tiger halted, Dylan just behind him. In the middle of the floor, a black-maned lion and Ben fought side-by-side against a horde of bloodsuckers. The *zilithal* had stripped out of their clothes to reveal bodies that were little more than skin stretched over muscular bone, emaciated but strangely strong at the same time. The bloodsuckers fought with swords and daggers, claws and teeth.

Ben swung a wicked-looking knife, striking, killing. Dylan fought as his lion, huge and deadly.

The *zilithal* weren't immortal, like vampires. They

were live creatures, bred in some hellhole, and they could die. Already the floor was littered with their bodies, which broke down rapidly into bones that slowly turned to dust.

One *zilithal* pulled out a sword so curved it looked like a scythe, got under Ben's reach, and struck hard. Ben's eyes widened, and with a tearing sound, he tumbled down, split in half. The top part of his body fell forward as the bottom part went backward in a wave of blood.

The collective *zilithal* went insane at the scent. They dove for Ben, but the lion was there, roaring and striking, defending the dead body of his friend.

Dylan watched in horror. "Stop it," he yelled at Tiger. "Do something."

Tiger only shook his head, his eyes filled with sadness. "We can't. We're out of time."

Dylan wasn't sure if he meant they were too late or they were outside time. Tiger didn't elaborate.

Tiger stood motionless, tears on his cheeks as he watched the destruction. Dylan believed him when he said they could do nothing—if Tiger could have acted, he'd have been all over the *zilithal* and wiped them out in seconds.

The only reason Dylan hadn't brought Tiger to the meet was that he hadn't wanted to take Tiger from his family on Yule.

No, two reasons. Arrogance was the second. Dylan thought he could face dangerous beings without much worry. He'd counted on his own skill at making people do what he wanted, sure the *zilithal* would negotiate and become Dylan's secret weapon.

Instead, Dylan had led Ben into a trap. These creatures were mindless, wanting only the kill.

But he could do nothing about it now. As he watched, the *zilithal* swarmed over the lion. Bodies flew as Dylan's huge paws batted them aside, but in the end, there were too many. The *zilithal* stabbed and clawed, bit and stabbed some more, until the lion fell to his belly, fighting all the way.

One sword made it to the lion's heart. He slumped forward, blood spilling from his mouth, his eyes clouding.

The Dylan standing by Tiger heard his last thoughts—*My sons, my mate, my family ... I'm sorry. And I love you.*

The bloodsuckers screamed their triumph. Then they fed. Within only a few minutes, the floor was cleared of blood, and Ben and Dylan were silent, drained corpses.

"I won't let this happen," Dylan whispered next to Tiger. "Let's go, lad. I've seen enough."

More than enough. Dylan wanted to be sick and

then fall to his knees and weep. He hadn't wanted to do that since ...

Tiger didn't move. Dylan opened his mouth to snap at him, then saw what he did.

Light flickered deep inside the ruined warehouse. As Dylan watched, it flared to life, a line of white that stretched from floor to ceiling.

A man stepped out of that light, one taller than most humans, and even many Shifters. He was thin, not massive like a Shifter, and his hair fell to his waist in white-blond braids. He wore furs over leather studded with silver, with a knife and sword hanging from his belt. The scent that came with him made Dylan's lips curl into a snarl.

Fae.

Only one. Dylan knew the warehouse rested on a ley line—he'd researched it—but he'd counted on that to give him an edge with the *zilithal*. Ben liked ley lines and grew stronger with them, even if he couldn't go through them to Faerie.

The Fae walked to Dylan's dead body. The lion had shifted back into human form after death, and Dylan saw his own face, pale and lifeless, blue eyes staring, the gray in his hair stark in the dim light.

Before the Fae reached the corpses, he halted, glancing toward Tiger and Dylan as though sensing something—as Tiger had when Zander had taken

Dylan to the Yule ceremony. The Fae looked puzzled, sniffed the air, and then turned back toward the bodies.

He took a small box from under his furs and opened it.

"No!" Dylan couldn't stop his shout.

The Fae didn't hear him. He gazed down at the dead Dylan and began chanting in the Fae language.

The Dylan on the floor groaned. A light shot upward from his chest and solidified next to the Fae— the dim outline of Dylan himself, dressed in jeans and leather jacket, blue eyes glaring fury.

"Gobshite," Dylan heard his other self whisper.

The Fae laughed, triumph on his face. He held the box toward the insubstantial Dylan, who dissolved into light and flowed into the box, cursing all the way.

The Fae snapped the box closed, held it up, and shouted a word that sounded like a cry of victory.

"Son of a fucking ..." Dylan rounded on Tiger. "He took my soul. No Guardian to send me to dust, and he was here in seconds. They're watching—waiting for me to die."

"Yes. You are valuable."

"Shite." Dylan paced back and forth, fists clenched so hard he cut into his own palms. "That's how they knew how to attack Shiftertown—how to win this war. They stole my soul and extracted my secrets. And Ben ..." Dylan gazed with sorrow at the fallen Ben, whose outline was slowly changing into the giant creature he truly was. A beast of Faerie, long-forgotten. "He was a key. And I threw him away. I threw away his *life*."

Dylan continued to pace, anguish, uncertainty, and self-anger pushing at him. "This hasn't happened yet, is that right? Can I stop this?"

Tiger said nothing, as enigmatic as ever.

The Fae finished his gloating and turned for the ley line, box held like a trophy.

"I *am* stopping this." Dylan spun, growls filling his throat, the lion inside him done with slow games. "He doesn't win."

He started after the Fae at a run, clothes falling as he shifted. His lion came down on all four paws just as the slit of light that was the ley line flared.

Dylan leapt with the ease of long experience, launching himself like a missile onto the Fae.

Dylan went right through him. The Fae and Dylan weren't in the same place and time, and could never touch.

The box in the Fae's hands flashed, Dylan's captured soul bursting out. It sought the Dylan outside time, recognizing its own essence, having no difficulty with the line between the real and the not.

The soul connected with the one inside the leaping Dylan, burning like the fires of the Yule log. Dylan roared in pain as white light seared him.

The light blotted out the Fae, who looked furious, the warehouse, the smell of death, and Tiger. The last thing Dylan saw was Tiger's golden eyes.

Then, nothing.

Dylan gasped as he tumbled down, and air poured into his lungs with the damp coolness of a Louisiana winter morning.

He sat straight up in bed in the haunted house, roaring his pain.

All was serene. Dylan was no longer on the floor, the bedroom whole and undamaged. Morning sunshine leaked through the curtains at the window. The odor of coffee drifted down the hall, along with the sound of Ben's off-key singing.

CHAPTER SIX

D ylan bounded up from the bed, grabbing shirt and jeans.

He could move, he could breathe, and his bedroom wasn't covered in fallen beams and ceiling plaster. The chandelier swayed, the crystals tinkling as Dylan hurriedly pulled on his clothes.

He raced down the hall, barefoot, and into the kitchen. Ben stood in front of the stove, stirring something in a frying pan, the coffee maker gurgling.

"Hey," Ben said over his shoulder. "Want breakfast? I'm doing omelets, have a mess of bacon ready to go, toast in the toaster."

"No."

At Dylan's abrupt word, Ben turned to him in curiosity, spatula in hand.

Dylan drew a long breath, taking in the familiar

and *normal* scents of coffee and breakfast foods. "What day is it?"

"Friday ..." Ben said cautiously. "The day after Thursday. The Winter Solstice. Tonight we meet with—"

"Meeting's cancelled."

Ben's dark brows went up. "The meeting we planned and sweated over all year? That meeting?"

"Yes." Dylan folded his arms, suddenly cold. The temperature had dropped, and he needed a sweatshirt. "It's a bad idea. They'll trap us and kill us."

"And you know this how?"

Ben's eyes showed perfect innocence, puzzlement, and a little annoyance.

"I had a dream," Dylan said. "Or a premonition. Or was given a vision. Something."

Ben nodded sagely. "That can happen in this house. Doesn't mean the vision is true."

"Not taking the chance. You and I are going back to Austin. Right now."

"Yeah? And what do we tell the hell-spawn we're recruiting to help us fight the Fae? You know, the ones who barely agreed to the meeting at all. Who will be pretty pissed off when we don't show up. They might plan a little retaliation."

"Contact them." Dylan moved to the coffee pot, which had finished dripping, and poured himself a cup. He'd need at least that fortification. "Tell them to meet us here instead."

"Here." Ben stared at him, as though convinced Dylan had lost his mind. "While we'll be ..."

"In Austin. No time to waste, lad. If we ride hard, we'll make it for the Yule celebration."

Ben gazed regretfully at the finished omelet in the pan then back at Dylan. He sighed. "All right, my friend. You're calling the shots on this one. But I'm pinning you down once we have a moment, and making you explain."

"I'll tell you everything. But not right now."

Dylan left Ben, who grabbed a fork and started shoveling eggs into his mouth straight from the pan. He returned to his bedroom and finished dressing, caught up his backpack, and headed downstairs.

At the bottom of the staircase, Dylan gazed up at the house above him. "Let the visitors in tonight," he told it. "And then do what you wish."

He wasn't certain the house would understand, but the ponderous chandelier that illuminated the wrap-around staircase swayed. A whisper of laughter touched Dylan, then dispersed.

Ben trundled down the stairs, a bag slung over his shoulder. "Can't say I'm sorry to trade a meeting with bloodsuckers for beer and burgers and hot Shifter women. Shall we depart?"

———

DYLAN AND BEN RODE INTO SHIFTERTOWN AS THE sun was sinking. Dylan parked his motorcycle in the drive of his house—which was solid and intact, the windows glowing with light. He stripped off his riding gloves and strode around the house to the clearing in back.

Ben followed, calling greetings to Shifters who were pouring from their homes, ready to light the Yule log. Shouts came back to them, filled with surprise and welcome.

Shifters parted as Dylan headed straight for Liam, who had a box of long matches in his hand, preparing to light the log after he said the blessing. Dylan reached his son and tackled him.

The unlit match spun from Liam's hand as he struggled not to fall. He and Dylan turned in an unsteady dance until son and father righted each other, Liam staring at Dylan in shock.

"Dad—"

The startled word cut off as Dylan slammed his arms around Liam in a hard embrace.

Liam's voice gentled. "Dad."

He pulled Dylan close. The power of touch, of family, flowed through Dylan and healed his heart.

The pain of the past, the horrors of the vision, began to melt away.

Another touch on Dylan's back, Sean. Drawn to the family huddle, he closed on Dylan from behind, joining in the comfort.

The group staggered as Connor smacked into them, holding on with surprising strength. Shifters started to say, "Awww," and then reach for their own mates and cubs.

Liam loosened his hold and wiped his eyes, though Sean and Connor clung to Dylan, connecting with the man who'd carried them through disaster and peril, life and death.

Kim was next to Liam now, Katriona in her arms. Kim's spirit and fearlessness, and most of all, her love, had calmed Liam and made him a happy man, as well as the great leader Dylan had known he would become.

Dylan turned to Kim and pulled her and Katriona into his embrace. Katriona reached out and patted her grandfather's head.

The pat was more of a smack, the little girl having Morrissey strength. Dylan chuckled and gave Katriona a kiss on the top of her head.

Andrea was next, her healing magic coming through her warmth. Dylan pressed his cheek to hers. "Take care of them," he whispered.

Andrea blinked, but seemed to understand.

Sean held baby Kenny, whom Andrea had handed off to him. The cub stared at Dylan in wolf-like satisfaction, and Dylan wondered if Kenny had truly seen him in the vision or dream, or whatever it had been.

Kenny grinned, breaking his usual solemnity. "Gan-da!" he proclaimed, and launched himself into Dylan's arms.

Glory hovered behind Sean as Dylan held Kenny, his heart wrenching as he thought of his son Kenny, dead and gone. As usual, Glory hesitated to intrude, but at the same time felt the pull to Dylan's family. Dylan reached for her and gathered her to his side.

Glory's eyes flickered, but she masked her surprise and slid a strong arm around him.

"What changed your mind?" she asked. "Dylan Morrissey decided family and friends were more important than his mission? Or did you have a flat tire or something?"

Dylan sensed Glory struggle between anger and elation. He tightened his hold on her as Andrea took Kenny from him, and he pressed a kiss to Glory's smooth cheek.

"Family is more important," he told her quietly. "And I can't do the mission alone. I won't save all Shifters single-handedly." He paused, letting his rare smile pull at his mouth. "No matter how much I want to."

"Dad admits he needs us." Sean punched the air. "Cause for celebration."

"This Yule log won't light itself." Liam shooed them away and picked up his dropped box of matches. "The Blessings of the Goddess be upon us!" he yelled into the crowd, struck a match, and touched its flame to the first branch.

The Shifters cheered. Connor, dancing on legs that grew longer each year, lit another. Then Sean, while Kim and Andrea held the cubs at a safe distance. Dylan moved to the log, his arm still around Glory, and held her hand while they both lit a branch.

Glory was trembling, probably with shock that Dylan was being so affectionate. But she'd put up with a lot of his shit, and he planned to make it up to her. Remembering their love-making in his vision, those plans for making up were starting to get him hard.

One more person to track down first. "Stay here if you want, love," he said. "I'll be right back."

"No, no." Glory twined her hand through his, her grip firm. "I'm not letting you go anywhere without me."

"Wise." Dylan wove through the Shifters who had started to shift, howl, sing, party.

Ben, naturally, led a conga line. Shifters kicked feet

and paws as they chanted and bounced around the Yule log and down the green. Ronan as a Kodiak bear doing the conga was something to see.

Dylan made for a ring of trees that always seemed to flourish in the center of the common. Standing against one was a Fae. His white-blond braids reached his knees, and he wore silk robes and furs similar to the ones worn by the Fae at the New Orleans warehouse. His black eyes glittered as he watched Andrea dance, Kenny in her arms. A bottle of Guinness rested in the Fae's long-fingered hand.

"Fionn," Dylan greeted him.

"Dylan." Fionn nodded at him, then Glory. "Thought you were off pursuing people to beat up and submit to your will."

"I was. That's off. Do me a favor."

Fionn Cillian, a warrior Fae who'd bested many other Fae in his part of that world, didn't do favors. But he and Dylan shared a grandson, and this counted for much. Fionn narrowed his eyes and waited for Dylan to continue.

"Stay diligent," Dylan said. "Fae will try to best you to get to us. There's a ley line in New Orleans in the old warehouse district—I'll give you the coordinates. Put a guard on it, or take over the territory behind it if you need to."

"Interesting." Fionn's eyes lit, as they always did

when he thought about battling someone. "Come to my tent and tell me about it."

His tent lay inside Faerie, through the ley line gate that rested in this grove. The tent was luxurious, filled with every comfort, including Fae-style whisky—very potent—and amazing food Fionn dismissed as army rations.

Glory stiffened at Dylan's side, expecting he'd go. Without her.

Dylan shook his head. "Tomorrow, my friend. It's Yule. Parties to go to, gifts to give, family to be with."

"Very well. I will wait." Fionn, who couldn't move much past the grove because of all the iron around, looked wistfully at Andrea. "Maybe the party could head this way?"

Shifters hated Fae in general, and not all of them trusted Fionn. But Dylan gave Fionn a nod. "It's done, mate. Good night."

Glory stared at Dylan in amazement as he led her back toward the house, but she said not a word. She also didn't let go of his hand.

Dylan gestured at Ben to take the conga line toward the grove. Andrea had already started for her father, carrying Kenny, Sean in her wake. Sean had left the Sword of the Guardian in the house, the symbol of death not needed in this celebration of life.

Dylan took Glory up the steps of their house, drew

her close for an intense kiss in the shadows of the porch, and then led her inside.

————

Motorcycles surrounded the empty house outside of New Orleans that Ben and Dylan had vacated that morning. The last *zilithal* streamed inside, joining the others in collective glee. They'd feast tonight on the blood of a Shifter and a goblin—the stupid fools.

The front door quietly closed, and just as quietly, the lock clicked. Silver moonlight brushed the old house and glittered on dark windows.

There was silence, and then a cacophony of screaming, and then nothing.

After a time, the door creaked open, and the house emitted a gentle burp.

————

Dylan lay entwined with Glory. They'd shared a wild hour or two, their shouts and groans filling the room.

Now they rested. Moonlight, the light of the Goddess, touched them, brushing Glory's beautiful body, locked against Dylan's.

The terror of Dylan's dream melted away. It would not happen, would never happen. The house, that devious piece of architecture, had given Dylan a Yuletide gift of the vision, explaining to him what was what.

Dylan was willing to learn the lesson. He fought not for renown or personal satisfaction—he did so to keep his family safe and gain their freedom. He realized that he couldn't do it alone, and only together would they prevail.

Glory studied him with beautiful gray eyes. If she looked a little smug, she deserved it. Dylan brushed back her golden hair and kissed her.

Outside, the revelry continued in its loud insanity. Shifters had much to celebrate, in spite of it all. The festivities shouldn't only be for tonight, Dylan decided. Every day should be a celebration of life and family, an opportunity to hold loved ones close as long as possible.

Including this beautiful, amazing Lupine in his arms.

"Penny for your thoughts," Glory murmured.

Dylan kissed her neck, then licked where he'd kissed. "I was thinking how much I loved you."

"Oh."

Dylan raised his head to find Glory watching him, a smile spreading across her face. "I love you too," she whispered. She gave him a sly look. "Want me to show you how much?"

"I'd never say no to that, love." Dylan kissed her deeply.

They wrapped themselves in each other once more, and soon the room resounded with their cries.

Moonlight bathed them in a soft glow as their voices blended with the laughter outside and flowed into the sparkling night.

AUTHOR'S NOTE

Thank you for reading!

While Dylan is the protagonist in this novella, it is **not** his final story. He will return in a full-length novel of his own, which traces his journey to his happily ever after.

The Shifters have come a long way since *Pride Mates* (Book 1, Liam and Kim's story). I remember having the first inkling of the series while driving past a construction site. I saw several good-looking men, one older than the others, and one younger, just out of his teens. My imagination put them into one family, three generations working together.

Then I thought—for no reason—what if they were Shifters? And the Morrissey family was born. They sprang into my head and began to act, and I wrote down what they did.

From the Morrisseys I moved to Shifters connected with them—Spike, Ronan, Ellison, and more—and began to explore Shiftertowns in Las Vegas, North Carolina, and Montana.

If you are new to the Shifters Unbound series, the best place to start is *Pride Mates* (Book 1), though each novel is a standalone, a single love story. I do my best to explain what is what as I go along, so even if you start in the middle of the series, you shouldn't get too lost.

There are now several communities of Shifters, and each have their own set of novels (though many cross over). I list them below for each community, in chronological order.

Austin Shifters

Pride Mates (Liam and Kim)

Primal Bonds (Sean and Andrea)

Bodyguard (Ronan and Elizabeth)

Hard Mated (Spike and Myka)

Lone Wolf (Ellison and Maria)

Tiger Magic (Tiger and Carly:
Tiger first appears in *Mate Claimed*, Las Vegas Shifters)

Feral Heat (Deni and Jace.
Jace crosses over from the Las Vegas Shifters)

Bear Attraction (Walker and Rebecca.
Crosses over to Kendrick's group)

Bad Wolf (Broderick and Joanne.
Briefly crosses with Montana Shiftertown)
Wild Things (Mason and Jasmine.
Intro of haunted house and Zander)
Tiger Striped (Tiger and Carly novella)
A Shifter Christmas Carol
(novella featuring Dylan)

Las Vegas Shifters
Wild Cat (Cassidy and Diego)
Mate Claimed (Eric and Iona)
Perfect Mate (Nell and Cormac)
Wild Wolf (Graham and Misty)

North Carolina Shifters
Mate Bond (Bowman and Kenzie.
Crossover with Las Vegas Shifters)

Kendrick's Group
(Most cross over with Austin Shifters)
Lion Eyes (Seamus and Bree)
White Tiger (Kendrick and Addison)
Red Wolf (Jaycee and Dimitri)

Montana Shifters
Guardian's Mate (Zander and Rae)

Note: I include Zander with the Montana Shifters, because Rae is from the Montana Shiftertown, but Zander moves between all the groups. It's his way.

New Orleans Shifters

Midnight Wolf (Angus and Tamsin.
Crosses over with Austin Shifters and Zander)

The character of **Ben** so far appears in *Wild Wolf, Mate Bond, White Tiger, Red Wolf,* and *Midnight Wolf*. He will also have his own book.

Check my website

https://www.jenniferashley.com

for additions as I continue to explore all the Shiftertowns!

Again, thank you for reading. I never dreamed how far the Shifters would take me, but it has been a wonderful journey!

All my best,

Jennifer Ashley

Shifters Unbound

Pride Mates

Primal Bonds

Bodyguard

Wild Cat

Hard Mated

Mate Claimed

"Perfect Mate" (novella)

Lone Wolf

Tiger Magic

Feral Heat

Wild Wolf

Bear Attraction

Mate Bond

Lion Eyes

Bad Wolf

Wild Things

White Tiger

Guardian's Mate

Red Wolf

Midnight Wolf

Tiger Striped

A Shifter Christmas Carol

Shifter Made ("Prequel" short story)

———————

Stormwalker

(w/a Allyson James)

Stormwalker

Firewalker

Shadow Walker

"Double Hexed"

Nightwalker

Dreamwalker

Dragon Bites

———————

ABOUT THE AUTHOR

New York Times bestselling and award-winning author Jennifer Ashley has written more than 85 published novels and novellas in romance, urban fantasy, and mystery under the names Jennifer Ashley, Allyson James, and Ashley Gardner. Her books have been nominated for and won Romance Writers of America's RITA (given for the best romance novels and novellas of the year), several *RT BookReviews* Reviewers Choice awards (including Best Urban Fantasy, Best Historical Mystery, and Career Achievement in Historical Romance), and Prism awards for her paranormal romances. Jennifer's books have been translated into more than a dozen languages and have earned starred reviews in *Publisher's Weekly* and *Booklist*.

More about Jennifer's series can be found at https://www.jenniferashley.com.

Printed in Great Britain
by Amazon

23647620R00051